Algernon Sydney Logan

Saul

A Dramatic Poem

Algernon Sydney Logan

Saul
A Dramatic Poem

ISBN/EAN: 9783337343316

Printed in Europe, USA, Canada, Australia, Japan

Cover: Foto ©Andreas Hilbeck / pixelio.de

More available books at **www.hansebooks.com**

A DRAMATIC POEM.

BY

ALGERNON SYDNEY LOGAN,

AUTHOR OF "THE MIRROR OF A MIND," "THE IMAGE OF AIR," ETC.

———————

PHILADELPHIA:

J. B. LIPPINCOTT & CO.

1883.

PREFACE.

As the view taken by the author of the relations between Saul and his subjects is not, perhaps, the most common one, a word or two in explanation seems requisite.

It is plain, from the Bible account, that the priests were very unwilling to grant the people's clamorous demand for a king. It seems probable that in selecting Saul, a poor shepherd boy, they chose one whom they thought it would be easy to mould to their will. On finding himself firmly seated on the throne, however, far from being pliant and yielding, he showed an evident intention of substituting kingly for priestly rule. A struggle thereupon began, which ended only with Saul's life. Steadily the quarrel increased in violence and fury until it culminated in Saul's putting to death great numbers of the lower order of priests, together with witches, prophets, and the like, as being the mouthpieces and agents of the higher priesthood. The natural answer to this was a declaration that the kingdom had passed from Saul, and the secret anointing of another, in order to give a figure-head to the clerical party. Warned by their past experience, the priests chose in David a youth of a deeply religious mind, in whom afterwards all their hopes and wishes were fulfilled.

It is uncertain whether the Philistines were induced to make their invasion by direct solicitation, or merely by the unsettled state of the kingdom. In any case, the presence of David in the Philistine camp, and the fact that he would have taken part with them in the battle against Israel had it not been for the doubts of the Philistines on the score of his fidelity, show very clearly that the sympathies of the sacerdotal party were with the invader.

The scorn that Michal felt for David's religious superstition, and which burst forth in after-years, when he danced before the ark,* is no small confirmation of my idea that their education had been as different as possible. And David's ungenerous and weak reply, when he taunts Michal with her father's downfall and his own elevation in his stead, shows plainly that David felt it was to the very bigotry which his wife despised that he owed his crown.

My clue to the character of Phalti is found in II. Samuel, chap. iii. 16.

The story of the last days of Saul, as told in the Old Testament, has enabled me to practically preserve the unities without effort. I have taken the

---

* II. Samuel, chap. vi. 14–22.

liberty of departing from the biblical text in so far only as to permit Saul's armor-bearer, in the last scene, to die before his master, and thus avoid a palpable anti-climax.

DRAMATIS PERSONÆ.

SAUL, King of Israel.

DAVID.

ABNER, Captain of the Host.

PHALTI, an officer.

JONATHAN,
ABINADAB, } Sons of Saul.
MELCHI-SHUA,

Ghost of Samuel.

MICHAL, Saul's daughter, who has been previously taken away from David, her first husband, by Saul, and given in marriage to Phalti.

The Witch of Endor.

Attendants, soldiers, etc.

The action of the drama is confined to Mount Gilboa and its immediate vicinity. Time, a single night and part of the following morning.

S A U L.

SAUL.

ACT I.

SCENE I.

Nightfall.—A lonely spot just within the Hebrew out-posts near Mount Gilboa.

Enter DAVID, *disguised as one of* SAUL'S *soldiers.*

DAVID.

'Tis strange that I, who had to pass the guards
And run all hazards, should be here the first.
What if my messenger mischanced! I fear
Lest ill hath come to Jonathan—for Saul
Hath long half doubted him—That cannot be,

Else were I taken—Hark!—It is a step—(*hides*).
I know that shadow—Jonathan!   'Tis I!

> *They embrace.*

JONATHAN.

Thy message reached me but an hour ago,
And scarcely could I find a fit excuse
To quit the council.   Anywhere but here
Thy sight were happiness, but thou must know
That to be taken here is certain death—
Why art thou come?

DAVID.

>   Thou knowest why I come.
Thou art my earliest and my dearest friend,
And shall I see thee sink beneath a doom
Which overhangs and topples o'er thy head,
And stretch no hand to pluck thee to my heart,
Where only there is safety?   Jonathan,
Twice hast thou saved my life from him who long

Has been the scourge of Israel, and now
I fain would save thee from him, that alone
He may receive the merit of—

JONATHAN.

No more!
I know thy wrongs are great, but so has been
The provocation,—not at first from thee—
Thy heart was far from the intentions vile
To thee imputed—Yet thou hast become
By slow degrees, through priestly influence,
The head and hope of all our factious foes.
How much I loved thee let this be the proof,
That I still love thee; for to see thee here
In open arms against us doth abate
Much of that girlish tenderness which made
Our boyhood's love a proverb to our friends.

DAVID.

Come with me, Jonathan!

JONATHAN.

I'll never come!

DAVID.

There is no time for argument, and yet
I do so fear to fail that I must plead—
Oh hear me, Jonathan, thou art allied
With one who is the enemy of God—
Fight not against the Lord, but fly the accursed!
Doomed from the day when Agag was not slain
At God's command, but blasted since he slew,
At Nob, Ahimelech, the holy priest,
And eighty priests beside—thou knowest his sins,
His heart-beats number them—Then fly with me!
'Tis noble to desert from wickedness.

JONATHAN.

Had other lips dared thus to speak of Saul
They ne'er had spoken more.—I'd have thee know

That Saul, 'if he were now, instead of king,

But a plain goatherd, would be still by far

The greatest man in Israel—

DAVID, *interrupting him.*

Why Ay,

The greatest—nay, for though thou just hast said

Thou lovest me no more, I would not wound—

The fate of all allied to thee is fixed,

But thine still quivers—pause while there is time,

Think ere too late—wilt thou not join us?

JONATHAN.

No.

DAVID.

Art thou then bound forever to this cause

Forecrushed of God?

JONATHAN.

For this most noble cause
I fight unto the death with all save thee.

DAVID.

And I with all save thee.—Adieu!

JONATHAN.

Adieu!

Exeunt severally.

SCENE II.

A house within the Hebrew lines.

SAUL (*solus*).

This restless hush, this lull before the storm,
Lies heavy on my spirit.   'Tis a time
Without a form, a very nondescript,
Too still for bustling self-forgetfulness,

Too close to tumult for the calm of thought.

My past seems unfamiliar—if I turn,

My Future is a name and nothing more.

The Future do we make our fixed abode,

While its uncertainties are scattered wide,

Accepting them as constant—but so soon

As they unite and crystallize, and form

A crisis near at hand, all things beyond

Are blotted from our sight by this great doubt—

We can but strive to cross it.

Enter ATTENDANT.

ATTENDANT.

                    Good my Lord,

The captain of the host awaits without.

SAUL.

Admit him.

                              Enter ABNER.

To ABNER.

　　　For the color of thy news
I see at best 'tis neutral, from thy face,
So do not preface it.

ABNER.

　　　　I have no news
In need of preface.　Watches have been set
Far out on all the roads.　I hear the foe
Is moving, and we soon shall know his mind.

SAUL.

Hast thou been forth amongst the tents, to learn
The temper of the men?

ABNER.

　　　　　Our tribe is staunch
Because it is our tribe—nay, all are firm,
They all will face the foe—But David is
Beloved in Israel.

SAUL.

Ay, there it is!

This pebble-throwing boy, this priestly tool,

This thing of songs, this curious piece of cloth

Whose warp is craft, whose woof is bigotry,

Has won the rabble's heart before that I

Could lift their minds above him.   Even now

They will not judge him, though he is arrayed,

An open rebel, with our enemies,

And on the march to slay his brethren.

ABNER.

Nay,

I hear he is not trusted by the foe,—

It is not certain he will fight with them.

SAUL.

It is as certain full as that he is

The cup from which the priests would hope to drink

This people's blood—their liberty—for that

Is their souls' blood.

ABNER.

         Our priests, my lord, are men
Of holy life—

SAUL, *not heeding him.*

         It maddens me to think
That should I fail, I shall go down to time,
Since priests are our historians, as the foe
Of my own people whom I lived to save,
Tricked out, besides, by sacerdotal hate.
It will be told how often I did come
To sue forgiveness, shedding many tears,
With ashes on my head, upbraiding loud
My froward heart.   Had I but been more swift
To catch and punish, letting none escape—
Had I forgotten always they were men,
In seeing they were priests, the tide had turned—
'Tis but a step 'twixt opposite beliefs!
But as it was, the few I left but gained

Strength fróm the slain, and skulked among the tribes,
The poison-mongering victims of their cause.

ABNER.

I never was a friend to many rites—
I am a plain man—yet I would not dare
Thus to revile our priests ; they are the link
Betwixt us and Jehovah.

SAUL.

It is time
You went to your own tent to take some rest—
We move at break of day—

Enter hurriedly a messenger.

MESSENGER.

My lord the King,
A body of the enemy is now
Moving towards the mountain, as it seems,
To occupy the heights.

SAUL.

It must not be.
The advantage of position is with us—
It shall not be! Abner, thou wilt draw out
A thousand chosen men for instant march—
Phalti shall lead them, and to save delay
I go to him, to give him my commands.

Exeunt.

SCENE III.

MICHAL'S *apartment in the same.* MICHAL *is seated,*
PHALTI *reclining at her feet.*

PHALTI.

Michal, my own, my darling, my beloved,
Fain would I linger here, and by thy side
Forget that ever there was war on earth.
It is enough to watch those amorous hands,
Veined to the very finger-tips ; and mark

Each easy, idle, half-voluptuous pose—
When one loves thus, 'tis almost death to go.

MICHAL.

Think that the cause you fight for is to you
Most holy, and that soon you may return
Loaded with honors, and enjoy them long.

PHALTI.

'Twere easier far to tear myself away
From passionate entreaties to remain—
To forcibly unwind thy close-locked arms,
And steel my lips to every clinging kiss,
Than to go thus in calm propriety,
With this cold, mother's blessing on my head.

MICHAL.

'Twould pain me much to think that I could stand
Betwixt you and your duty.

PHALTI.

There it sounds!
This self-same note forever in my ears!
Duty thou art thyself, personified—
Forever calm, obedient to my will,
Wanting in nothing—save in being part
Of my whole life, and heart, and inmost soul.

MICHAL.

Long have I striven to be all you wish.

PHALTI.

We feel no need to strive when once we love.
I hoped to slowly, surely win my way—
'Tis not so now—I see the distant goal
No nearer than at first—You love me not.

MICHAL.

Phalti, you do me wrong.

PHALTI.

It may be so—
But still I do not see you deeply blush
When I come in, and pale when I depart.

MICHAL.

Push me no further—I cannot control
The mounting and descending of my blood.
To love you is my duty—

PHALTI.

What, again?
Accursed be the phrase, I almost said
Cursed be the lips that uttered it!   And thou!
Dost thou suppose I deem thee so demure,
So cold, so calm, so breezeless?   Nay, I know
Passion is there, too much, though not for me—
I know thy idle longings where they run.
And is it not enough that thou hast come
Straight from that renegade, that rebel—?

B   3

MICHAL.

Stop!
Trench not upon the past, or I may prove
That I can wake and speedily atone
For all my past docility—

PHALTI.

And I
Will prove my might, which fondness has con-
cealed.

Enter SAUL.

SAUL.

Phalti, away! There is no time for words.
Go straight to Abner's tent; there thou wilt find
Men, guides, directions—Occupy and hold
The heights on Mount Gilboa.

PHALTI.

Yes, my Lord.

Exit PHALTI.

SAUL.

Would more were like thee, Phalti! If I had

But a few score such soldiers, ere the moon

Can light yon mountain side my foes were dead,

All cut to pieces in a night surprise,

And that vile rebel—But I have them not—

And so, dear Michal, do I turn to thee,

Thee, a weak woman, yet my flesh and blood,—

And therefore in thee only shall I find

That sympathy with me and all my aims,

That reflex of my thoughts, which I must have.

Abner is but a soldier, and the rest

Are cowed by priestcraft into doubt and fear.

But I have formed thy mind, and I have forged

All thy soul's weapons for the war of life.—

Now, for I scorn concealment, when my fate,

Our fate, our cause stands in most desperate
     doubt,

The cause I've taught thee in our happy walks,

The cause I live for, I come home to thee—

Give me a hearty wish for my success,
And hurl a curse upon my enemies.

MICHAL.

You say most truly that you formed my mind,
I could not think against you if I would—
A handiwork must act within the laws
Of him who framed it.   Need is none to ask
My mind's support, it is already yours.
Your cause is just, since surely it is right
To check the dark dominion of the priests—
And yet a cloud upon my spirit hangs,
I walk confused within a misty maze.
It seems to me there is some strange mistake,
That could you only meet with some of those
Who now oppose us, you would find them far
Less stubborn than you deem, that they would see
The splendor of your majesty and might,
And hasten to obey—Oh, think what joy
To be once more united all in love!

SAUL.

Your husband, it would seem, has little part
In these your dreams of happiness to come.
There is a ring of treason in your words.

MICHAL.

There is no treason to you in my heart.

SAUL.

Then prove it straight by calling ruin down,
Signal, complete destruction, upon all,
Without distinction, who oppose me now.

MICHAL.

May the Philistines suffer rout.

SAUL.

                   Well done!
I marvel at your warmth in my behalf!
What, as I entered, was the cause of strife

Betwixt you and your master, my beloved,
My well-tried Phalti?

MICHAL.

        Ask my master that—
Lord Phalti best can tell on his return.
He was complaining, if my memory serves,
That I was far too meek and dutiful.

SAUL.

Lord Phalti! And you will not curse my foes!
Then naught remains for me but now to hurl
My curse on you; and tell you, since your heart
Is with that rebel, I will pluck it thence,
Though I uproot you with it, root and branch!

                            Exit SAUL.

ACT II.

SCENE I.

A moonlight balcony.

SAUL (*solus*).

Of all the shadows midnight and the moon
Upon me cast, none equals that within.
Would it were always night, a moonless night,
And I and all men isolated parts
Of universal shadow.—What are men?
Vain children plucking at the sleeve of Time,
Who stalks away unheeding. Once I deemed
The world was made for me to revel in.
Beauty was life's wide atmosphere, the breath
And essence of existence, ne'er to fail.
Joys poured so thick upon me, that my soul
Feared only lest, with all her granaries,

She could find room through life but for the tithe.

But soon I made a grand discovery—

That life was labor, and still happier so,

That happiness sprang only from renown,

And naught could satisfy, save leading men.

My sensual dream was fair, and if, indeed,

Its colors faded when too closely scanned,

It still gave pleasure ; but ambition's dream

Was deadly, for within me lurked success.

Although those near in blood and far in heart

Tramped o'er the garden of my soul, it still,

By Obstinacy tended, bloomed the more.

But happiness before me flitted on ;

For when the shepherd boy had won the throne,

Another vista opened out beyond,

And a new goal, though this time more defined.

I longed to turn my studies to account,

And make a nation of disjointed tribes ;

To stifle superstition, and teach men

To be themselves the judges of their lives.

And still the more my thoughts grew absolute,

And abstract, and unpliable, the more

I deemed mankind were following close with me,

Till insurrection shook me by the arm,

And I awoke, and found myself alone.—

What is it to be in a wilderness?

Its thickly whirling leaves, or blowing sands

Speak with eternal voices—But to be

Alone in thought, to bear a gift to men,

And be waved off by every heart in turn,

Is desolation.   To escape the frowns

Of those around me, I could wish my heart

Were leprous as their own.   Wrapped in great
        thoughts,

From lack of sympathies, I shrank from men—

What agony to see them shrink from me!

Had I but loved the beings whom I saw!

Yet no one ever loved both man and men.

Then why not make my utter loneliness

But serve my greatness?   It were nobler, sure,

c

To find in enmity the very oil
To make my zeal burn brighter than before—
A hundred times repeated, still the words
Sound cold and dead, and quickly float away,
Like echoes on the wind.   Man cannot live,
Noble or vile, without the love of man.
All strive for it, and strive for that alone,
Beneath a thousand names and thousand masks.
A few of us, more daring than the rest,
Finding but little ready to our hand,
Pluck from the clouds the vapors of our choice,
And in far-flashing but uncertain tints
Trick out the wraith we call Posterity.
We clasp our misty doll, a moment glad—
But fading soon, it takes the ashen hue
Of all things else, and mingles with the air,
And leaves us staring stupidly around
For aught to clutch at, looking but in vain.

A sentinel passes, chanting slowly.

The world's asleep—
Sleep on !
My watch I keep
Alone.
Toil, care, and crime
Take breathing time—
Sleep on !

These varied phrases will not lift one flint
Of all the mountains pressing on my back.
So strong the sense of my identity,
From inward isolation, that it seems
That all the world must live or die with me.
E'en Time upon me lays his withered hand,
And moves but as I move, and holds me back—
Forever-more beside my hapless steps
Walk sorrow, mad confusion, and despair !

Sentinel repasses, singing.

Hearts o'er the world,
Care's sails are furled,
Sleep on !

I vigil keep

That ye may sleep—

Sleep on !

Leaves shuddering lisp

On high,

Ghastly the wisp

Hops by,—

Yet do not fear,

Sweet rest is here,

Vexed heart, thy troubles cease;

Sorrows, away !

Till break of day—

These be the signs of peace.

My mounted wishes I on foot pursue,

Their doubling tracks my guide across the waste;

But now their very traces disappear,

And I am doubting if they ever were

Aught but the hurrying squadrons of a dream.

A second sentinel passes, singing.

The first watch wanes; the moon now dim,
Now bright, is sailing high—
The first watch wanes, night's swallow grim
In the moonlight eddies by.

Is it so late?   'Tis time that they were here,

My messengers returning from their search—

A noble search!   I hear their steps—Come forth!

(*knocking heard within.*)

Enter an attendant.

To attendant.

Well, have ye found the witch?

ATTENDANT.

We have, my Lord.

A shepherd showed us where the sorceress,

Not far from Endor, dwells within a cave

High on the mountain; to the foot from here

Is scarce an hour's ride—Shall we then send

A squad to take her?

4

SAUL.

No, I go myself.
I long have felt a wish, or rather whim,
From merest curiosity, to see
Some witch like this, of real force and fame,
In her own den, begirt with all her spells.—
Haste, bring the steeds.   We must be back before
The dawn's first pale, sleep-smothered blush appear.

Exeunt attendants.

So wild a venture upon such a night,
The headlong gallop and the dizzy climb,
And all so close to the Philistine lines,
Will clear my brain and set my nerves at rest.

Exit.

SCENE II.

A mountain near Endor.   Time, midnight.   SAUL and
two attendants mounting upward.

SAUL.

The white and shected ghosts of the dead storms
Sweep by in majesty! and all around
The trees' dark branches seem to beckon me;
And near my path their rough and twisted roots,
Like coiled-up serpents, seem about to hiss;
And even the shadows, those most shapeless things,
Take living shapes about my fevered steps (*looking*
    upward).
Ye curling forms fantastical aloft,
Is it that hanging thus 'twixt earth and sky
I feel your influence, or are the sprites
Which now I seek, though unbelievingly,
Part of this stable world as well as I?

ATTENDANT, *coming up from below*.

My liege, we pray you hold! you climb so swift
That we, though straining, fall behind—we fear
To lose you in the darkness.

SAUL.

                              Ye are slow.
Yet will I pause upon this jutting crag
Whose edge invites me to its crumbling brink—
'Tis a most dizzy rock—beneath I see
The red and dotted camp-fires of our host,
Like fire-flies in the amorous month of June,
Flash as the breezes lift them.

ATTENDANT.

                              My good lord,
If it should please you, we will hasten on,
And strive to find the entrance to this cave.

SAUL, *not heeding him.*

A feather falling from such height 'twould seem

Might crush a tower to atoms.   Far away,

Across the wide and lake-besprinkled plain,

The moonbeams kiss the waters into life

As radiant as their own.   This glimpse beyond

The world that lives in contact with our steps,

This sudden outlook on a wider scene,

Blots out my narrow life of strife and pain;

Conspiracy and priestcraft, civil broil,

Shrink to their wraiths, and now become to me

But quaint, cold names of things of long ago.

My pristine purity, my early thoughts,

The passionate thoughts of heaven-gazing Youth,

Which soared aloft and left me in those days,

On reascending, lo! I find them here.

Why have I made them wait for me till now?

Let me believe reality is dead—

It seems so here—that I am once again

A boy upon Mount Ephraim, these pure beams,

4*

These shadows, and this lofty solitude,
My childhood's playfellows—

ATTENDANT, *from above.*

My Lord the King,
I pray you hang not o'er yon treacherous cliff,
Lest it should crumble.   We but now have found
The cavern you are seeking—please you, come.

SAUL.

Push on, I follow.   Your unmeaning tongues,
Your thoughtless babble, checking this fair scene,
Are, for the moment, the deep voice of Fate.

Exeunt.

SCENE III.

*A cavern in the mountain, arranged as an abode.
The* WITCH OF ENDOR (*sola*).

WITCH.

Weary and lone, weary and lone.   Alas !
How many nights in perfect loneliness,

And utter desolation, have I sat

In this grim haunt which even the hunter shuns!

How often have I left my door of boughs

Half open, that the bats which dwell with me

Might come and go!—this is to be alone.

I, feeble, timid, and oppressed with years

Which I can scarcely reckon—I who need

The peaceful fireside, and the gentle hands

Of my descendants for my ministers,

Am driven hither by the fear of death,

To live a life far worse than death—What crime

Have I committed?—Is this criminal,

That at long intervals I have beheld

Shapes from the past and listened to the dead,

Becoming thus the mouth-piece of the tomb?

O Saul, O Saul, thou slayer of the priests

And scorner of the prophets, thou who hast

Destroyed my order, what wouldst thou perform?

Hopest thou to choke the accents of the grave?

The spirits speak not yet, but still I hear

Low whisperings, and I know thy hour is nigh—
Thy retribution comes—alas! alas!
Our nation's fortunes are with thine entwined.

Voices without, and sound of steps.

Oh God! they come to take me! Whither hide?
What, to be dragged forth like a badger? No!
Let them come on, I meet them here—Approach,
    (to those without)
Whoe'er ye be, I wait within.

Enter, disguised, SAUL *and attendants.*

SAUL, *to his two attendants.*

                Keep watch
And careful guard without 'gainst treachery.

They retire.

To the Witch.
Woman, whate'er thou art, thou sure must be
Or good, or ill, and this is, in itself,
No small distinction in this neutral world
Where few are either. I have heard thy fame,

And that to thee there is no past—I come
To exercise thy calling; and no time
Is mine to waste in prefaces—Call up,
From out eternity, the shape of him
Whom I shall name to thee.   Nay, haste!

WITCH.

My Lord—

For though I know you not, your mien is high—
Come not to lay a snare for my old life,
It is not worth your pains.   You know how Saul
Hath cut off all the wizards, and all those
Who dealt in witchcraft; therefore now depart,
Tempt me no farther, I would fain descend
Unsmeared with gore to my impatient grave.
'Tis now the only boon I ask of man.

SAUL.

It boots thee not to know who I may be—
But I possess great power with the king,

And now I swear that by the Lord of Hosts,
The God of Israel, no harm shall come
To thee for aught thou docst—haste, proceed !

WITCH.

Whom shall I call, my Lord ?

SAUL.

Call Samuel.

WITCH.

Mighty prophet, from thy deep,
Dreamless, everlasting sleep,—
Even from nothingness awake,
And thy perished form retake.

Let such thoughts as need but soul
Join to make thy phantom whole—
Let my will transfused through thee
Gift thee with identity.

By'the Covenant, and by
Its mighty ark of victory,
By the name which Hebrews prize,
Wake, dread spirit, wake, arise!

A pause.

SAUL.

Woman, thy earnestness might shake the doubt
Of weaker minds—What, hast thou seen a shape?

WITCH, *not hearing him.*

Dim forms are rising, even as when the wind,
That vacillating sculptor, shapes the clouds,
Each form, half moulded, he in turn destroys
To rear the following—here are figures wild,
In gestures threatening, and in aspect fierce,
Yet most indefinite.

SAUL.

What see'st thou now?
Speak quickly, for my heart is in my throat.

WITCH.

'Tis changed, 'tis changed! an old man cometh up
Wrapped in a mantle, full of majesty—
The phantom mutters—Nay—O thou art Saul!
Oh, spare my life!

Shade of SAMUEL *appears.*

SAUL.

Peace, woman, thou art safe.
Grim shade of one in life most grim and stern,
But doubly ghastly now, I charge thee speak!

SHADE OF SAMUEL.

Why hast thou broke my trance, and called me back
To memory and pain?

SAUL.

O Samuel!
Despite thine order, thou wert once my friend;
And now when all, all whom I then did trust

Have turned my foes, be thou, though in the tomb,

Again a friend—Oh, speak some word of cheer!

Give me thy counsel what 'twere best to do.

With lukewarm troops, and hourly thinning ranks,

I must oppose the great and eager host

Of the Philistines—I am in despair.

That black, arch rebel, Jesse's son, hath joined

The forces of the foe; and gives it out,

False villain that he is, that even by thee

He was anointed.   I can find no help

In visions, or in dreams, or prophecies—

(Things which I once did scorn, but covet now)

Oh, speak to me! say, whither shall I turn?

What shall I grasp at?

SHADE OF SAMUEL.

                        Wherefore come to me,

Seeing the Lord has left thee?   Jesse's son,

Whom thou despisest, is to-night the king,

And thou a king but in our chronicles.

Because thou wouldst not execute God's wrath

On Agag, king of Amalek, this doom

Has fallen on thee.   Furthermore, the Lord

Will Israel with thee deliver up

(Slaughtering his people to make way with thee,)

Into the hands of the Philistine host.

Thy joys and hopes, thy beauty and thy strength,

Thy friendships, and thy pleasures, and thy peace,

Thy better moments, and thy happier thoughts

Are in the past, and thou upon its verge.

To-morrow shalt thou be what I am now—

A terror unto all things, save thyself—

A concrete part of that great abstract, Death—

That one great mote which turns man's sight to

      tears,—

That dread negation, and that dull mistake.

Farewell! we part, I to my sullen sleep,

Thou to thy shuddering passage to the tomb.

     As SAUL *falls fainting to the earth the scene*

     closes.

ACT III.

SCENE I.

MICHAL'S *apartment.*

MICHAL (*sola*).

'Tis past the midnight hour, and yet methinks
I ne'er shall sleep again.—Their bitter taunts
At last have roused my soul, and fevered thoughts
In answer to their challenge come in crowds.
Phalti and Saul, if that ye had been wise,
Ye had not asked for more than I can give;
Or asking it, and seeing me in doubt,
Striving to live, yet longing but to die,
Ye had not sought to force the gates of love
By wearisome upbraidings or abuse.
A woman rarely wishes to be loved—
Misers at once and prodigals they are:

All love they fain would hold within themselves,

To squander all where least there is a chance

Of just return.   And thus it is with me.

Had Phalti's been a less uxorious love,

Less constant and, I shame to own, less pure—

Perchance—But no, it might not, could not be!

I could not still be living, and forget

That beauty and that strength which taught me
        love—

Taught me to languish, and to die of joy,

My pulse to flutter, and my breath to fail—

Taught me to cease from thinking and to live!

O life all sense, all passion, and all soul,

O life of mad excitement full of rest,

'Twere better far to die than longer live

Without thee!   Peace, wild heart, be still!

Think how that life was sapping to the mind,

Think—think of aught to help allegiance back!

Father, my duty surely is to thee,

What should I be, deprived of thy support?

Thou gavest me life, and hast endowed my mind,

And yet, since thou art father to my woes,

Perchance I owe thee naught—I cannot tell.

My conscience says that I should strive to feel

The worth of Phalti's love, that I should lean,

As once I leant, upon my father's arm—

And yet this is the most that I can do:

In sullen silence to tramp on alone;

Now turning back and gazing wistfully,

Now staggering on, instinctive, at the call

Of one or both; with mind and senses chilled,

With wavering heart, not fixed in either faith—

A breathing type of human misery.

Oh, it would help me in my bitter woe,

To know a day was coming, though so far

It should but seem a rear-ward speck of dust

Of the long caravan which ages lead

Across this desert world—a time when love

Might walk the earth, unchained and unreproached,

When woman's person might but follow free
Where'er her heart was guiding—Ah, I fear
This wingless, footless hour will come to us
No sooner than when Truth fantastical
Has grown a substance,—Sorrow a dim shade,—
Vain-longing ceased to be sustaining food,—
Death grown a harlequin, and Time a sloth.

Enter female attendant.

ATTENDANT.

My lady, have you heard the dreadful news?

MICHAL.

No, speak, what news?

ATTENDANT.

Perchance it is not true.

MICHAL.

I charge thee, by the Eternal, speak!

ATTENDANT.

Indeed,

It may not all be true—Pray do not look
So deadly pale—

MICHAL.

Speak now! unless—unless
You wish to see me die—

ATTENDANT.

Oh, hear it then!
They say there has been fighting near the heights,
And that he has been taken, if not slain.

MICHAL.

He, who?

ATTENDANT.

Lord Phalti, who else could I mean?

MICHAL.

Why keep me in such mad suspense and dread?
For I had thought—I mean I cannot tell—
I am bewildered—tell me all again.

ATTENDANT.

There's nothing more to tell.

MICHAL.

                    Did you not say
Lord Phalti had been slain?

ATTENDANT.

                    Taken, or slain.

MICHAL.

Tell me more facts.—Did other leaders fall—
Leaders of our, or of the other side?

ATTENDANT.

None that I know of, lady—None, I think.

MICHAL.

I am bewildered—Leave me all alone—
Yet stay within my call.

ATTENDANT, *aside.*

This heavy blow
Has stunned her and benumbed her senses quite.

Exit attendant.

MICHAL.

Freedom is freedom still, though bathed in blood!
This moment, out of all Eternity,
Is mine!   The Past has risen from the grave!
I hear *his* voice—What answer shall I make?
Yes—No—yes—no—I must not, it is wrong—
Wrong!   It is treason!   Give me time to think.
Away with thought!   Thought has but wrecked my
        soul.
Unsought the plan springs up before my mind.
Is it inspired, or is it but a black
And foul temptation?   She will think I go,
Half crazed by grief, and led by wifely love,
To search for Phalti—When once past the lines!
Help, I am dizzy, help!

The attendant enters and offers aid.
Commanding herself.

'Tis almost past,—

It was a moment's faintness, that is all.

Go to the sentry whom I lately saw

Pacing beneath my window—Give him now

All thou canst carry—offer him besides—

Worlds, should he ask them !   Stick at nothing, so

He will consent to help us through the lines.

ATTENDANT.

Think of the peril, think how vain the search,

If my Lord Phalti has been taken—

MICHAL.

Go !

But one word more, one breath may cost thee—Go !

Exit attendant.

Oh father, grieve not, think me not unkind,

Thou never wert so dear to me as now.

I go to draw thee to the one I love,

And him to thee; or failing that, to strive

To mitigate your violence.—And now (*goes to a*
   burnished mirror)

I leave thee, father, this poor lock of hair,

As a remembrance, till we meet again ;

To show thee I depart in perfect love,

And in the hope—What madness !—Even now

I feel his eye consume me—'Tis in vain ! (*sinks into a*
   seat.)

Attendant re-enters.

ATTENDANT.

The sentinel consents to let us pass.

MICHAL, *starting up.*

And help us ?

ATTENDANT.

Yes.

MICHAL.

Pass on before, I come.

Exit attendant.

I cannot go—I cannot stay—and yet—
To feel his breath once more upon my cheek,
To pant upon his bosom—and then die!
O David, master, husband, I am thine!

Exit.

SCENE II.

A desolate moonlit pass. A pale streak visible in the east. Enter MICHAL *wearily. Throws herself down at the foot of a rock.*

MICHAL.

I can no more, and yet I still must on.
It all seemed plain and easy at the start;
When with unwearied limbs and soul unlost
I left my sheltering room, no longer mine.

I was, by some impossibility,

To be a link of love 'twixt two opposed

And mighty beings, both of whom I love.

I strove to be the bridge between two high

And frowning crags—I hurled myself across,

And have but fallen into the abyss

Which yawns between, that gulf, black, bottomless,

Through which I still am falling.   What are limbs

Aching and bruised, and flint-chopped, bleeding feet,

And fevered head, beside the tired soul—

The dizzy, lost and homeless soul?   Alas!

My freedom is but liberty to die;

For how can I before the man I love

Appear a foot-sore, draggled suppliant,

A wandering outcast, and a traitor, too?

I who was—Oh, it cannot be! and soiled,

Soiled in his eyes since those delicious days

When I was his, all his—Down, down, vile self,

Thou cold slug that dost sting the tree of life

Till it puts forth deformities.   To doubt

6

The being I adore is base—I go (*rising*)
To seek him, trusting only to his love,
E'en though I should fall dead before his tent
Of weariness and shame—

Enter PHALTI, *wounded.*

Who's there?   Ah!
She falls with a shriek to the earth.

PHALTI.

See,
'Tis only I—No foe is near—'Tis I,
Phalti, thy husband—Wake, belovèd, wake!

MICHAL.

It is some hideous dream—Oh pardon!   Oh,
Let us part quickly ne'er to meet again—
But not in wrath—though I have done thee wrong,
Much have I suffered.

PHALTI

Thy poor mind is dazed
By the mad fever of fatigue.   Forgive!
'Tis easy to forgive one loved before
For this, that she has nobly fronted death,
And suffered hardship, just to search for me,
Who am not worthy to be found alive.
But if I live 'tis from necessity :
When all was lost I thought by my own hand
To die; but in a moment more I flung
My sword over the precipice, and shame
Kindled my cheek to think that I had planned
To make my death my screen, and slink away
From my plain duty to the King.   In war
Misfortune is a crime.   Saul did not say,
"Take thou the heights if those with thee prove
       true,
And bravely do thy bidding," but he said,
" Phalti, go thou and occupy the heights,

And hold them." I have failed—And now I go
To pay with my poor life this failure. Come!
My hours are numbered; and when I am gone
('Tis hard to say), perchance thy lot will be
Brighter and happier—Darling, come away.
Rest dost thou need, and I will lead thee straight
To thy fond father's arms—

MICHAL.

Not there! not there!
Oh let me go, I say! Or kill me now!
Thou goest to death—and what is death beside
The thought of standing 'neath my father's eye?
To have him call me traitor, whom I love,
And tear my passion from my breast with scorn,
And trample it all bleeding under foot—
My love is thine, and I will worship thee
With heart and soul and sense and every nerve,
If thou wilt only let me go!

PHALTI.

This night
Has shattered thy poor nerves and turned thy brain.
Rest only can restore and calm thy mind;
Even against thy will thou must with me—
Come, dearest, come, I bear thee hence to peace.

> *Exit, bearing with him the half struggling,*
> *half fainting* MICHAL.

SCENE III.

MICHAL'S *apartment.*

SAUL, *at the open window.*

The misty grays and violets of the dawn,
Last lingering remnants of the quiet night,
Are dying one by one, and in the east
The blood-red hue of this combative day
Comes flashing up and staining all the world.
The saddest is to think an hour hence

I shall enjoy the carnage, and be made
To undergo the influence I hate,
And imitate the stupid violence
Of the vile cause I combat.   Fade away,
Fade sober tints, pure colors of the soul,
My clear, my mind-appealing cause must bear
The brutal arbitration of the sword.
First of the suns, if prophecy be true,
That shall behold my world a blank to me,
Thy rising which should bring me solemn thoughts,
Speaks only of the march, and nothing more.—
Strife never seemed so hateful as to-day,
Nor wrath so senseless; and yet here it was
I parted from my child with bitter words,
Unjust to her, the only one I love.
Michal, come forth!   I know I did thee wrong,
I have but little to forgive, and thou
Hast more than I would own to—Hasten, child,—
Nay, do not sulk, indeed there is not time.
Thou hast been sharer in my inmost thoughts,

And now that we must part, and part, perchance—
Come, bid me speed—

An attendant enters.

ATTENDANT.

What would my Lord the King?

SAUL.

Thou must have heard—I would the princess—Go!

ATTENDANT.

The princess is not here—that is—I mean—
The captain of the host is here, my Lord.

SAUL.

What means this stuttering bewildered fool?

Enter ABNER.

Abner, where is my daughter?

ABNER.

She is fled.

Shall we pursue?

SAUL.

Ay, take her, if you will.
Set all the camp to grinding of their swords—
There's time enough, they need not quit their lines—
Tell them to sharpen to a wire-edge,
'Twill soonest reach the bone.   Before thy tent
Bid Melchi-shua and Abinadab
And all the captains meet me, to receive
My final orders ere we storm the heights.

Exeunt.

SCENE IV.

The camp.

SAUL, ABNER, ABINADAB, MELCHI-SHUA, JONATHAN
(*apart*), *and captains.*

SAUL.

Captains, I have no flowers of speech for you,
No exhortations, no haranguing words

Of general meaning.   All of you I know,

And love and trust you all.   To-day we fight

For freedom; since this black Philistine host

Comes at the call of a vile faction, who

Would barter national liberty for power,

And fix a cursed oligarchy here,

A secret, dark and mystic tyranny;

Trampling to death that natural government,

That secular, free, open, mutual rule

Which ye yourselves have chosen.—Scale the
     heights!

Take quick advantage of each bush and twig—

Creep, shield your bodies with each jutting stone;

And when with care and toil ye gain the top,

Cut not your enemies, but pierce them through,

Exposing not your persons.   And be sure

Where'er the steam of blood shall thickest rise,

Fantastically curling up on high,

There in the midst, like lightning in a cloud,

Shall ye behold the flashings of my blade.

And now farewell! Ye know your posts—Advance!
Abner, go with them—Soon we meet with joy,
Or meet no more.

ALL, *drawing their swords.*

Farewell!

Exeunt, except ABINADAB, MELCHI-SHUA, *and*
JONATHAN.

SAUL, *to* ABINADAB *and* MELCHI-SHUA.

Come here, my sons.
Ye two and Abner I can wholly trust;
But many of the captains are not sure,
And should the day go heavily with us,
Close in upon the wings, and swiftly lead
Your little remnants up to join with mine,
That we may make one push for victory,
Or perish side by side.

ABINADAB.

Yes, father.

SAUL.

Go!

Exeunt ABINADAB *and* MELCHI-SHUA.

To JONATHAN.

Some whom I most have trusted, Jonathan,
Have proved unworthy; should the converse hold,
Thou, whom I oft have doubted, now shouldst be
Our chief support.

JONATHAN, *advancing.*

Try me, my Lord.

SAUL.

But if,

In thick of fight, the man I would not name
Who has been made the nucleus of this storm,
Should meet thee, wilt thou kill or capture him?

JONATHAN.

The man you mean is not now with the foe.

SAUL.

Where heard you that? You know too much—
      Depart!
Keep near Abinadab throughout the fray,
And do your duty.

JONATHAN.

You shall see, my Lord.

Exit.

SAUL.

She cannot hope for mercy, if brought back—
Could she not wait till I was in my grave!
And Phalti, too! but he at least is dead,
And she will not be taken while alive.
'Tis much to know I ne'er shall see them more.

Enter MICHAL, *supported by* PHALTI

Phantoms, away!   Accursed shadows, flee!

One have I wronged, yet both have me betrayed!

I dread ye not—Begone!

MICHAL, *feebly*.

Alas! my Lord,

We are not phantoms yet—Oh would we were!

SAUL.

I scarce can tell, ye look so worn and wan,

So inorganic, effortless and strange,

Ye seem but forms of human agony.

Things which a falling dew-drop might engulf,

Or gossamer might strangle, or the breeze

Dissolve, diffuse, and mingle with the air.

Curses I had for one of you, and death

Perchance for both, yet who can curse or kill

A lifeless shade which pain doth animate?

Speak, if ye may.

PHALTI.

My master, I am come
To offer up my life, of little worth,
Save as a pledge of my fidelity,
Now forfeit through my failure.

SAUL.

Get thee gone!
Thou hast destroyed our cause, and ruined me,—
Thy sight is hateful,—yet I do not know
Of one just reason for thy death—Begone!

PHALTI.

Scarce need I recommend to your kind care
My wife, your daughter, whom I lately found
Searching for me within the pass—

SAUL, *interrupting him.*

Why, ay,
She searched for thee, and hoped to find thee dead,
And, dead or no, to slake and satiate
Her frantic passion for thy foe—At last

Thou goest forth, uncertain, dizzy, blind,

Drunk with thy sorrow.

Turning to MICHAL.

But where goest thou?

There is no place in Heaven or Earth for thee.

Help, some one, help! She falls! Michal, my child!

Michal, my darling—Ah! 'tis but a swoon—

I thought her dead.—Thou hast the self-same look

Thou hadst that day in childhood when I found

Thee sleeping softly by the rivulet,

Thy tiny hand still grasping tiny shells,

And thy hair crowned with weeds—No more I see

The passionate kisses of my enemy

Upon thy altered lips. If thought there be

After this life—within the land of shades,

Purged of thy passion, be thou unto me

Companion of Eternity! Farewell! (*a distant trum-*
   pet sounds.)

   As SAUL *rises from his knees and moves away,*
   the scene closes.

SCENE V.

Mount Gilboa.

Sounds of battle and pursuit. Enter SAUL *and his armor-bearer, both mortally wounded.*

ARMOR-BEARER.

Here may we pause. Behind these rocks we stand
Out of the current of the flying—

SAUL.

                        Ay!
Out of the current of the world we stand—
Time hath passed by us, leaving me to creep
As best I may, into my bloody grave.

ARMOR-BEARER.

There is no hope for any of us now.

SAUL.

My sons are dead—all three—Abinadab
Died fighting desperately when all his wing
Were broken, mixed and flying; after him
Fell Melchi-shua, noble in despair;
And Jonathan, whom I did half suspect,
Died best of all in that last furious charge
Which almost saved our fortunes.—

ARMOR-BEARER.

Hark! I hear
The sound of horses' hoofs.

SAUL.

It is the foe
Close on the heels of those who passed just now—
I would not die by these Philistine dogs—
Take thou this sword and hold it steadily—
Nay, hold it true—for I have had enough
Of suffering already.

7*

ARMOR-BEARER.

My good Lord,
I am bewildered—There, will this then do?

Holds the sword feebly.

SAUL.

What, trembling so?

ARMOR-BEARER.

I cannot help it—no,

Lets fall the sword.

I cannot do this deed—I do not know
Whether it be because thou wert the King—

SAUL.

I *was?* nay, thou art right, I was the King.

ARMOR-BEARER.

It may be these deep wounds—for I am faint—
I cannot see thee, Saul, this dizziness—

Faints and dies.

SAUL.

Now I am left to finish it alone.

Mere pain were nothing—But to kill the world

Of thoughts within, collected through long years,

Result of toil, of pleasure, and of pain—

A world so multitudinous that I

Think only of the havoc I must make!

Pauses.

Why should I writhe thus—am I not alone?

The sounds of the pursuit have swept afar,

And left me like a stranded broken shell.—

It is so silent and so peaceful here

The time seems altered, and the work quite done,

And Saul and all his miseries a tale

Heard long ago in childish years, as told

In dreamy accents o'er a hearth of coals,

Whose shapes fantastic acted out the play—

My mind is wandering, yet I cannot now

Command it back to face reality.

The myriad tribes and peoples of the earth, (*delir-*
    iously)

A writhing mass of passions, efforts, wills,

With only love of self distinct and clear,

That cause of all their good and all their woe,

Calm, passionless, removed, I see them now,

As the much-pondering, absent-minded moon

Looks down upon the nations of the clouds.

             Sounds of the Philistines close at hand.

The bitterness is back again!   Away!

                    Falls upon his sword.

My thoughts disband, for they are homeless now.

                             Dies.

www.ingramcontent.com/pod-product-compliance
Lightning Source LLC
Chambersburg PA
CBHW030002030726
47499CB00008B/2862